I0648218

William Allingham

Rhymes for the Young Folk

William Allingham

Rhymes for the Young Folk

ISBN/EAN: 9783337273996

Printed in Europe, USA, Canada, Australia, Japan

Cover: Foto ©Andreas Hilbeck / pixelio.de

More available books at **www.hansebooks.com**

CONTENTS.

LIST OF ILLUSTRATIONS.

THE FAIRIES.

Up the airy mountain,
    Down the rushy glen,
We daren't go a-hunting
    For fear of little men ;
Wee folk, good folk,
    Trooping all together ;
Green jacket, red cap,
    And white owl's feather !

Down along the rocky shore
    Some make their home.
They live on crispy pancakes
    Of yellow tide-foam ;
Some in the reeds
    Of the black mountain-lake,
With frogs for their watch-dogs,
    All night awake.

15

High on the hill-top
  The old King sits;
He is now so old and gray
  He's nigh lost his wits.
With a bridge of white mist
  Columbkill he crosses,
On his stately journeys
  From Slieveleague to Rosses;
Or going up with music
  On cold starry nights.
To sup with the Queen
  Of the gay Northern Lights.

They stole little Bridget
  For seven years long;
When she came down again
  Her friends were all gone.
They took her lightly back,
  Between the night and morrow,
They thought that she was fast asleep,
  But she was dead with sorrow.
They have kept her ever since
  Deep within the lake,
On a bed of flag-leaves,
  Watching till she wake.

By the craggy hill-side,
  Through the mosses bare,
They have planted thorn-trees
  For pleasure here and there.

Is any man so daring
    As dig them up in spite,
He shall find their sharpest thorns
    In his bed at night.

Up the airy mountain,
    Down the rushy glen,
We daren't go a-hunting
    For fear of little men ;
Wee folk, good folk,
    Trooping all together ;
Green jacket, red cap,
    And white owl's feather !

An Elf sat on a twig,
He was not very big,
He sang a little song,
He did not think it wrong;
But he was on a Wizard's ground,
Who hated all sweet sound.

Elf, Elf,
Take care of yourself!
He's coming behind you,
To seize you and bind you,
And stifle your song.
The Wizard! the Wizard!
He changes his shape
In crawling along,
An ugly old ape,
A poisonous lizard,
A spotted spider,
A wormy glider,
The Wizard! the Wizard!
He's up on the bough,
He'll bite through your gizzard
He's close to you now!

The Elf went on with his song,
It grew more clear and strong,
    It lifted him into air,
        He floated singing away,
    With rainbows in his hair ;
While the Wizard-worm from his creep
        Made a sudden leap,
        Fell down into a hole,
And, ere his magic word he could say,
    Was eaten up by a Mole.

THE FAIRY KING.

"High on the hill-top
The old King sits:
He is now so old and gray
He's nigh lost his wits."

THE Fairy King was old.
He met the Witch of the Wold.
"Ah ha, King!" quoth she,
"Now thou art old like me."
"Nay, Witch!" quoth he,
"I am not old like thee."

The King took off his crown,
It almost bent him down ;
His age was too great
To carry such a weight.
"Give it here!" she said,
And clapt it on her head.

Crown sank to ground ;
The Witch no more was found.
Then sweet spring-songs were sung,
The Fairy King grew young,
His crown was made of flowers,
He lived in woods and bowers.

CHORUS OF FAIRIES.

Golden, golden,
Light unfolding,
Busily, merrily, work and play,
In flowery meadows,
And forest shadows,
All the length of a Summer day!
All the length of a Summer day!

Sprightly, lightly,
Sing we rightly,
Moments brightly hurry away :
Fruit-tree blossoms,
And roses' bosoms,—
Clear blue sky of a Summer day!
Dear blue sky of a Summer day!

Springlets, brooklets,
Greeny nooklets.
Hill and Valley, and salt sea-spray,
Comrade rovers,
Fairy lovers,—
All the length of a Summer day
All the livelong Summer day!

ROBIN REDBREAST.

GOOD-BYE, good-bye to Summer!
  For Summer's nearly done;
The garden smiling faintly,
  Cool breezes in the sun;
Our Thrushes now are silent,
  Our Swallows flown away,—
But Robin's here, in coat of brown,
  With ruddy breast-knot gay.
Robin, Robin Redbreast,
  O Robin dear!
Robin singing sweetly
  In the falling of the year.

Bright yellow, red, and orange,
  The leaves come down in hosts;
The trees are Indian Princes,
  But soon they'll turn to Ghosts;
The scanty pears and apples
  Hang russet on the bough,
It's Autumn, Autumn, Autumn late,
  'Twill soon be Winter now.
Robin, Robin Redbreast,
  O Robin dear!
And welaway! my Robin,
  For pinching times are near.

The fireside for the Cricket,
    The wheatstack for the Mouse,
When trembling night-winds whistle
    And moan all round the house ;
The frosty ways like iron,
    The branches plumed with snow,—
Alas! in Winter, dead and dark,
    Where can poor Robin go ?
Robin, Robin Redbreast,
    O Robin dear,
And a crumb of bread for Robin,
    His little heart to cheer.

AMY MARGARET.

Amy Margaret's five years old,
Amy Margaret's hair is gold,
Dearer twenty-thousand-fold
      Than gold, is Amy Margaret.

"Amy" is friend, is "Margaret"
The pearl for crown or carkanet?
Or peeping daisy, Summer's pet?
      Which are you, Amy Margaret?

A friend, a daisy, and a pearl;
A kindly, simple, precious girl,—
Such, howsoe'er the world may twirl,
      Be ever,—Amy Margaret!

JINGLE, JANGLE!

JINGLE, jangle!
Riot and wrangle!
What shall we do
With people like you?
Here's Jingle!
There's Jangle!
Here's Riot!
There's Wrangle!
Never was seen such a turbulent crew!

You, north must go
To a hut of snow;
You, south, in a trice,
To an island of spice;
You, off to Persia
And sit on a hill,
You, to that chair
And be five minutes' still!

DREAMING.

A STRANGE little Dream
On a long star-beam
Ran down from the midnight skies,
To curly-hair'd Fred
Asleep in his bed,
With the lids on his merry blue eyes.

Under each lid
The thin Dream slid,
And spread to a picture inside,
A new World there,
Most strange and rare,
Tho' just by our garden-side.

Rivers and Rocks,
And a Treasure-Box,
And Floating in Air without wings,
And the Speaking Beast.
And a Royal Feast,
My chair beside the King's;

A Land of Flowers,
And of lofty Towers
Carved over in marble white
With living Shapes
Of Panthers and Apes
That gambol in ceaseless flight;

And a Cellar small
With its Cave in the Wall
Stretching many a mile underground!
And the Rope from the Moon!—
Fred woke too soon.
For its end could never be found.

I LOVE YOU, DEAR.

I LOVE you, Dear, I love you, Dear,
You can't think how I love you, Dear!
    Supposing I
    Were a Butterfly,
I'd waver around and above you, Dear.

A long way off I spied you, Dear,
No bonnet or hat could hide you, Dear,
    If I were a Bird,
    Believe my word,
I'd sing every day beside you, Dear,

When you're away I miss you, Dear,
And now you're here I'll kiss you, Dear,
    And beg you will take
    This flow'r for my sake,
And my love along with this, you Dear!

SEASONS.

In Spring-time, the Forest,
  In Summer, the Sea,
In Autumn, the Mountains,
  In Winter,—ah me!

How gay, the old branches
  · A-swarm with new buds,
The primrose and bluebell
  Fresh-blown in the woods,
All green things unfolding,
  Where merry birds sing!
I love in the Woodlands
  To wander in Spring.

What joy, when the Sea-waves,
  In mirth and in might,
Spread purple in shadow,
  Flash white into light!
The gale fills the sail,
  And the gull flies away;
In crimson and gold
  Sets the long Summer Day.

O pride! on the Mountains
    To leave earth below;
The great slopes of heather,
    One broad purple glow;
The loud-roaring torrent
    Leaps, bound after bound,
To plains of gold Autumn,
    With mist creeping round

Ah, Wind, is it Winter?
    Yes, Winter is here;
With snow on the meadow,
    And ice on the mere.
The daylight is short,
    But the firelight is long;
Our skating's good sport;
    Then story and song.

In Spring-time, the Forest,
    In Summer, the Sea,
In Autumn, the Mountains,—
    And Winter has glee.

THE CAT AND THE DOG.

THERE once lived a Man, a Cat, and a Dog,
And the Man built a house with stone and log.
" If you'll help to take care of this house with me,
One indoors, one out, your places must be."
Said both together, " Indoors I'll stay !"
And they argued the matter for half-a-day.

"Come, let us sing for it !" purrs the Cat;
"No !" barks the Dog, " I won't do that."
"Come, let us fight for it !" growls Bow-wow; ·
"Nay !" says Pussy, "mee-ow, mee-ow !"
"Well, let us race for it !"—said and done.
The course is mark'd out, and away they run.

Puss bounded off; the Dog ran fast;
Quickly was Puss overtaken and pass'd ;
But a Beggar who under the hedge did lie
Struck the poor Dog as he gallop'd by
A blow with his staff, and lessen'd his pace
To a limp : so Pussy won the race.

The Beggar went on his way to beg ;
Dog was cured of his limping leg ;
And Cat keeps the inside of the house,
Watching it well from rat and mouse,
Dog keeps the outside, ever since then,
And always barks at beggar-men.

CP

HERE AND THERE.

(A JUVENILE CHORUS.)

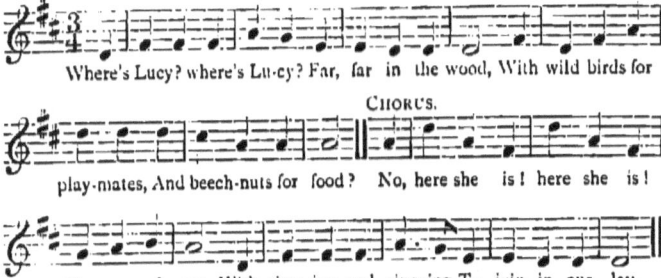

Where's Lucy? where's Lu-cy? Far, far in the wood, With wild birds for

CHORUS.

play-mates, And beech-nuts for food? No, here she is! here she is!

Hap-py and gay, With sing-ing and ring-ing To join in our lay.

Where's Gerald ? where's Gerald ?
　　He's out in the snow ;
The stars shining keenly,
　　The cold wind doth blow.

No, here he is ! here he is !
　　Happy and gay :
With singing and ringing
　　To join in our lay !

Where's Evey ? where's Evey ?
　　She's lost in the fog ;
Go seek her, go find her,
　　With man and with dog.

No, here she is ! here she is !
　　Happy and gay ;
With singing and ringing,
　　To join in our lay !

Where's Henry ? where's Henry ?
　　Poor Henry's afloat ;
The sea-waves all round him,
　　High tossing his boat.

No, here he is ! here he is !
　　Happy and gay ;
With singing and ringing
　　To join in our lay !

Where's Charley ? where's Charley ?
  In China dwells he ;
He wears a long pig-tail,
  Perpetually drinks tea.

> *No, here he is ! here he is !*
>   *Happy and gay ;*
> *With singing and ringing,*
>   *To join in our lay !*

Where's Johnny ? where's Johnny ?
  In Nubia, I know ;
He has climb'd a tall palm-tree,—
  A lion's below.

> *No, here he is ! here he is !*
>   *Happy and gay ;*
> *With singing and ringing,*
>   *To join in our lay !*

Where's Mary ? where's Mary ?
  Young Mary's asleep ;
And round her white pillow
  The little dreams creep.

> *No, here she is ! here she is !*
>   *Happy and gay ;*
> *With singing and ringing,*
>   *To join in our lay !*

Where's Bertha? where's Bertha?
She has wings—she can fly!
She has flown to the bright moon—
Look up there and spy!

No, here she is! here she is!
Happy and gay;
With singing and ringing,
To join in our lay!

[AD INFINITUM.]

40

THE BIRD.

" BIRDIE, Birdie, will you pet ?
Summer-time is far away yet,
You'll have silken quilts and a velvet bed,
And a pillow of satin for your head !"

" I'd rather sleep in the ivy wall ;
No rain comes through, tho' I hear it fall ;
The sun peeps gay at dawn of day,
And I sing, and wing away, away !"

" O Birdie, Birdie, will you pet ?
Diamond-stones and amber and jet
We'll string for a necklace fair and fine
To please this pretty bird of mine !"

" O thanks for diamonds, and thanks for jet,
But here is something daintier yet,—
A feather-necklace round and round,
That I wouldn't sell for a thousand pound !"

" O Birdie, Birdie, won't you pet ?
We'll buy you a dish of silver fret,
A golden cup and an ivory seat,
And carpets soft beneath your feet !"

" Can running water be drunk from gold ?
Can a silver dish the forest hold ?
A rocking twig is the finest chair,
And the softest paths lie through the air,—
Good-bye, good-bye to my lady fair !"

WISHING.

Ring-ting! I wish I were a Primrose,
A bright yellow Primrose blowing in the Spring!
　　The stooping boughs above me,
　　The wandering bee to love me,
The fern and moss to creep across,
　　　　And the Elm-tree for our king!

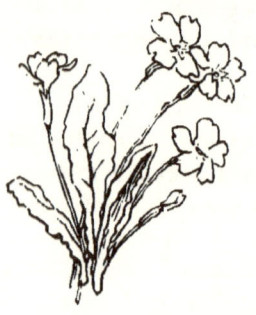

Nay—stay! I wish I were an Elm-tree,
A great lofty Elm-tree, with green leaves gay!
　　The winds would set them dancing,
　　The sun and moonshine glancing,
The Birds would house among the boughs,
　　　　And sweetly sing!

O—no! I wish I were a Robin,
A Robin or a little Wren, everywhere to go ;
　　Through forest, field, or garden,
　　And ask no leave or pardon,
Till Winter comes with icy thumbs
　　　　To ruffle up our wing.

Well—tell! Where should I fly to,
Where go to sleep in the dark wood or dell?
    Before a day was over,
    Home comes the rover,
For Mother's kiss,—sweeter this
              Than any other thing!

I SAW A LITTLE BIRDIE FLY.

I saw a little Birdie fly,
    Merrily piping came he ;
"Whom d'ye sing to, Bird ?" said I ;
    "Sing ?—I sing to Amy !"

"Very sweet you sing," I said ;
    "Then," quoth he, "to pay me,
Give one little crumb of bread,
    A little smile from Amy."

"Just," he sings, "one little smile ;
    O, a frown would slay me!
Thanks, and now I'm gone awhile,—
    Fare-you-well, dear Amy !"

A MOUNTAIN ROUND.

(Tyrol.)

Take hands, mer-ry neighbours, for danc - ing the round !
Moonlight is fair and de - li -cious the air ; From val - ley to
val - ley our mu- sic shall sound, And star - tle the wolf in his
lair. From sum- mits of snow to the for - est be -
- low, Let vul - ture and crow hear the e - choes, O -
- ho ! ;O - ho !) While sha - dow on mea - dow in
danc - ing the round Goes whir - li - g'g, pair af - ter pair !

Dal segno presto.

47

THE LEPRACAUN;

OR,

FAIRY SHOEMAKER.

I.

LITTLE Cowboy, what have you heard,
　　Up on the lonely rath's green mound?
Only the plaintive yellow bird
　　Sighing in sultry fields around,
Chary, chary, chary, chee-ee!—
Only the grasshopper and the bee?—
　　　" Tip-tap, rip-rap,
　　　Tick-a-tack-too!
　　Scarlet leather sewn together,
　　　This will make a shoe.
　　Left, right, pull it tight;
　　　Summer days are warm;
　　Underground in winter,
　　　Laughing at the storm!"
Lay your ear close to the hill.
　　Do you not catch the tiny clamour,
　　Busy click of an Elfin hammer,
Voice of the Lepracaun singing shrill
As he merrily plies his trade?
　　　He's a span
　　　And a quarter in height.
Get him in sight, hold him tight,
　　　And you're a made
　　　Man!

You watch your cattle the summer day,
Sup on potatoes, sleep in the hay:
   How would you like to roll in your carriage,
   Look for a Duchess's daughter in marriage?
Seize the Shoemaker—then you may!
     " Big boots a-hunting,
       Sandals in the hall,
     White for a wedding-feast,
       Pink for a ball.
     This way, that way,
       So we make a shoe;
     Getting rich every stitch,
       Tick-tack-too!"
Nine-and-ninety treasure-crocks
This keen miser-fairy hath,
Hid in mountains, woods, and rocks,
   And where the cormorants build;
     From times of old
     Guarded by him;
     Each of them fill'd
     Full to the brim
       With gold!

III.

I caught him at work one day, myself,
   In the castle-ditch where foxglove grows,—
A wrinkled, wizen'd, and bearded Elf,
   Spectacles stuck on his pointed nose,
   Silver buckles to his hose,

Leather apron—shoe in his lap—
　　" Rip-rap, tip-tap,
　　　　Tack-tack-too!
　　　(A green cricket on my cap!
　　　Away the moth flew!)
　　　Buskins for a fairy prince,
　　　　Brogues for his son,—
　　　Pay me well, pay me well,
　　　　When the job is done!"
The rogue was mine, beyond a doubt.
　I stared at him, he stared at me;
　"Servant, Sir!"　"Humph!" says he,
And pull'd a snuff-box out.
He took a long pinch, look'd better pleased,
　The queer little Lepracaun;
Offer'd the box with a whimsical grace,
Pouf! he flung the dust in my face,
　　And, while I sneezed,
　　　Was gone!

　Raths, very ancient forts or entrenched dwelling-places, usually on hills;
the remains of these are common in Ireland and resemble what are called
" Rings" in England.
　Yellow bird, the yellow bunting, or " yorlin."

YES OR NO?

Yes or No?
Stay or Go?
He never can tell, he never will know!
We must not wait,
We'll all be late,
While Barnaby puzzles his queer little pate!

What do you say?
Off and away!
Make up your mind to go or to stay.
Fix on your plan,
Step out like a man,
And follow your nose as fast as you can!

SLEEPING.

Do all your sleeping at night,
For then niddy-noddy is right ;
    But awake you must keep.
    And it won't do to sleep,
In the middle of broad daylight.

The sun at the end of the day
Takes his mighty great candle away ;
    A curtain on high
    Is drawn over the sky,
And the stars peep thro' if they may.

There's the curtain of night over all,
There's our own window-curtain so small,
    And least in their size,
    Over Emily's eyes
Her fringed little eyelids will fall.

She kneels at the side of her bed,
And softly her prayers are said;
    Now, a kiss, my Dear;
    Come, Angels, near,
And keep watch round the little one's bed.

A SWING SONG.

Swing, swing,
Sing, sing,
Here's my throne, and I am a King!
Swing, sing,
Swing, sing,
Farewell earth, for I'm on the wing!

Low, high,
Here I fly,
Like a bird through sunny sky;
Free, free,
Over the lea,
Over the mountain, over the sea!

Up, down,
Up and down,
Which is the way to London Town?
Where, where?
Up in the air,
Close your eyes, and now you are there!

Soon, soon,
Afternoon,
Over the sunset, over the moon;
Far, far,
Over all bar,
Sweeping on from star to star!

No, no,
Low, low,
Sweeping daisies with my toe.
Slow, slow,
To and fro,
Slow——
    slow——
        slow———
           slow.

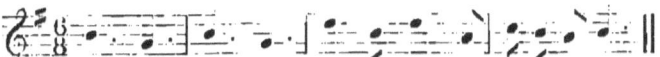

Swing, swing, sing, sing, Here's my throne and I am a King!

Swing, sing, swing, sing. Fare-well, earth, for I'm on the wing!

BIRDS' NAMES.

Of Creatures with Feathers, come let us see
Which have names like you and me.
Hook-nosed Poll, that thinks herself pretty,
Everyone knows, of all birds most witty.
Friendly Daw, in suit of gray,
Ask him his name, and ' Jack !' he'll say.
Pert Philip Sparrow hopping you meet,
" Philip ! Philip !"—in garden and street.
Bold Robin Redbreast perches near,
And sings his best in the fall of the year.
Grave Madge Owlet shuns the light,
And shouts " hoo ! hoo !" in the woods at night.
Nightingale sweet, that May loves well,
Old Poets have call'd her Philomel,
But Philomelus, *he* sings best,
While *she* sits listening in her nest.
Darting Martin !— tell me why
They call you Martin, I know not, I ;
Martin the black, under cottage eaves,
Martin the small, in sandy caves.

Merry Willy Wagtail, what runs he takes!
Wherever he stops, his tail he shakes.
Head and tail little Jenny Wren perks,
As in and out of the hedge she jerks.
Brisk Tom Tit, the lover of trees,
Picks-off every fly and grub he sees.
Mag, the cunning chattering Pie,
Builds her home in a tree-top high,—
Mag, you're a terrible thief, O fie!

　　Tom and Philip and Jenny and Polly,
Madge and Martin and Robin and Willy,
Philomelus and friendly Jack,—
Mag the rogue, half-white, half-black,
Stole an egg from every Bird;
Such an uproar was never heard;
All of them flew upon Mag together,
And pluck'd her naked of every feather.
" You're not a Bird!" they told her then.
" You may go away and live among men!"

DOWN ON THE SHORE.

I.

Down on the shore, on the sunny shore !
  Where the salt smell cheers the land ;
  Where the tide moves bright under boundless light,
    And the surge on the glittering strand ;
Where the children wade in the shallow pools,
  Or run from the froth in play ;
Where the swift little boats with milk-white wings
  Are crossing the sapphire bay,
And the ship in full sail, with a fortunate gale
  Holds proudly on her way ;
Where the nets are spread on the grass to dry,
And asleep, hard by, the fishermen lie,
Under the tent of the warm blue sky,
With the hushing wave on its golden floor
    To sing their lullaby.

II.

Down on the shore, on the stormy shore !
  Beset by a growling sea,
Whose mad waves leap on the rocky steep
  Like wolves up a traveller's tree :

Where the foam flies wide, and an angry blast
    Blows the curlew off, with a screech ;
Where the brown sea-wrack, torn up by the roots,
    Is flung out of fishes' reach ;
And the tall ship rolls on the hidden shoals,
    And scatters her planks on the beach ;
Where slate and straw through the village spin,
And a cottage fronts the fiercest din
With a sailor's wife sitting sad within,
Hearkening the wind and the water's roar,
    Till at last her tears begin.

THE BUBBLE.

See, the pretty Planet!
    Floating sphere!
Faintest breeze will fan it
    Far or near;

World as light as feather;
    Moonshine rays,
Rainbow tints, together,
    As it plays;

Drooping, sinking, failing,
    Nigh to earth,
Mounting, whirling, sailing,
    Full of mirth;

Life there, welling, flowing,
    Waving round;
Pictures coming, going,
    Without sound.

Quick now! be this airy
    Globe repell'd!
Never can the fairy
    Star be held.

Touch'd—it in a twinkle
    Disappears!
Leaving but a sprinkle,
    As of tears.

NICK SPENCE.

NICK SPENCE, Nick Spence,
Sold the Cow for sixpence!
  When his Master scolded him,
    Nicky didn't care.
Put him in the farmyard,
The stableyard, the stackyard,
  Send him to the pigsty,
    And Johnny to the fair!

AMBITION.

THE Sea! as smooth as silk,
And the froth of it like new milk,
And the sky a wonderful blue,
The cliff harebells have it too,
And scatter'd all over the shore
A thousand Children or more!

Suppose we join, one-will'd,
A City of Sand to build,
With a rampart broad and strong
From rock to rock along,
Solid and firm enough
To last till the sea grows rough
And the days turn chilly and short,
The end of our seaside sport,
When all must bundle and pack
And swift in the train go back,
Big folk and little folk,
To London lamps and smoke?

Let's draw out our plan to-night,
Begin it with morning light.
We'll bring all the Children together
And build in the sweet sunny weather.
What use in a House of Sand?
But a City—that *would* be grand!
O yes, I am sure it will stand!
And I, who first thought of the thing,
Perhaps they will make me King?

THE BALL.

ALL men, black, brown, red, yellow, white
Are brethren in their Father's sight.
To do each other good is right,
But not to wrangle, steal, or fight.

A thousand millions, young and old,
Some in the heat, some in the cold,
Upon this Ball of Earth are roll'd
Around the Sun's great flame of gold.

And this great Sun is like indeed
One daisy in a daisied mead ;
For GOD's power doth all thought exceed.
And of us also He takes heed.

RIDING.

His Lordship's Steed
Of a noble breed
Is trotting it fleetly, fleetly,
Her Ladyship's pony,
Sleek and bonny,
Cantering neatly, neatly.

How shall they pass
The Turf-Cadger's Ass,
Creels and all, creels and all?
Man on him bumping.
Shouting and thumping,
Heels and all, heels and all!

Lane is not wide,
A hedge on each side,
The Ass is beginning to bray;
"Now," says my Lord,
With an angry word,
"Fellow, get out of the way!"

"Ha!" says the Cadger,
As bold as a badger,
"This way is *my* way too!"
Says the Lady mild,
And sweetly smiled,
"My Friend, that's perfectly true."

The Cadger look'd round,
Then jump'd to the ground,
And into the hedge pull'd Neddy.
"O thank you!" says she,
"Ax pardon!" says he,
And touch'd his old hat to the Lady.

His Lordship's Steed
Of a noble breed
Went trotting it fleetly, fleetly,
Her Ladyship's pony,
Sleek and bonny
Cantering neatly, neatly.

The Cadger he rode
As well as he could,
Heels and all, heels and all,
Jolting and bumping,
Shouting and thumping,
Creels and all, creels and all.

TOM CRICKET

TOM CRICKET he sat in his hole in the wall,
    Close to the kitchen fire,
Up and down ran the Cockroaches all,
Red coats and black coats, great and small;
" Ho, Tom! our hearts are set on a ball,
    And your music we desire!"

Tom sat in his hole, his horns hung out.
    He play'd away on his fiddle:
The Cockroaches danced in a rabble rout,
Scrambling and scurrying all about,
Tho' they had their own steps and figures no doubt,
    Hands across, and down the middle.

Till, " Stay!" says a Fat One,—" We're no Elves,
    To dance all night without stopping!
Now for supper!"   They help'd themselves,
For the servants were gone to bed; on shelves
And tables they quested by tens and twelves,
    And quick to the floor kept dropping.

72

As a Cockroach ran by, says Tom Cricket to him,
　　" Fetch me up a piece of potato,
Good Sir!— to mix in the crowd I'm too slim.'
Says Jack Cockroach, " I see you are proud and prim ;
To eat alone is merely your whim,—
　　Which I never will give way to!"

" Come down," says he, " and look out for your share !"
　　" I won't do that," says Tom Cricket.
And when for another dance they care,
And call upon Tom for a lively air,
They find he has drawn himself back in his lair.
　　" How shameful," they cry, " How wicked !"

" Let's fill up the mouth of his cave with soot,
　　Because he's behaved so badly !"
They ran up and down the wall to do't ;
But ere half-done　a dreadful salute !
In came the Cook, and the Scullion to boot,
　　And off they all scampered madly.

THE YEAR OF HARDSHIPS.

JANUARY,
Bitter, very!
February damp, Sir;
March blows
On April's nose.
May has caught the cramp, Sir;
June,
Without a sun or moon!
July, August,
Many a raw gust;
September, October, November, December,
Ten times worse than I ever remember.
No apples, or hay, or honey, or corn;
I'm sure it wasn't a fat year.
Whenever you and I were born,
Good-luck it wasn't in *that* year!

A RIDDLE.

What I say you'll scarce believe,
Yet my words shall not deceive.
I saw what seem'd a little Boy,
With a face of life and joy;
He danced, he ran, he nodded, he smiled.
Just like any other Child;
But could not speak, (how strange was this!)
Or cry, or breathe, nor could I kiss,
To save my life, the cherry red
Of lips, not living and not dead!
He was no picture, statue, doll;
He was not a Child at all;
He was Nothing, as near as could be,
He was as real as you or me.
—There he is: turn and see!

Illustrated, Fine Art, and other Volumes.

Art, The Magazine of. Yearly Volume. With about 500 choice Engravings from famous Paintings, and from Original Drawings by the First Artists of the day. An Original Etching forms the Frontispiece. 16s.

Art Directory and Year-Book of the United States. With Engravings. 7s. 6d.

Along Alaska's Great River. By FREDERICK SCHWATKA. Illustrated. 12s. 6d.

American Academy Notes. Illustrated. 2s. 6d.

Animal Painting in Water Colours. With Eighteen Coloured Plates by FREDERICK TAYLER. 5s.

After London ; or, Wild England. By RICHARD JEFFERIES. *Cheap Edition,* 3s. 6d.

Artist, Education of the. By E. CHESNEAU. Translated by CLARA BELL. 5s.

Bimetallism, The Theory of. By D. BARBOUR. 6s.

Bismarck, Prince. By C. LOWE, M.A. 2 Vols., demy 8vo. With 2 Portraits. 24s.

Bright, Rt. Hon. John, Life and Times of. By W. ROBERTSON. 7s. 6d.

British Ballads. 275 Original Illustrations. Two Vols. Cloth, 7s. 6d. each.

British Battles on Land and Sea. By JAMES GRANT. With about 600 Illustrations. Three Vols., 4to, £1 7s. ; Library Edition, £1 10s.

British Battles, Recent. Illustrated. 4to, 9s. Library Edition, 10s.

Browning, An Introduction to the Study of. By ARTHUR SYMONDS. 2s. 6d.

Butterflies and Moths, European. By W. F. KIRBY. With 61 Coloured Plates. Demy 4to, 35s.

Canaries and Cage-Birds, The Illustrated Book of. By W. A. BLAKSTON, W. SWAYSLAND, and A. F. WIENER. With 56 Fac-simile Coloured Plates, 35s. ; half-morocco, £2 5s.

Cannibals and Convicts. By JULIAN THOMAS ("The Vagabond"). 10s. 6d.

Cassell's Family Magazine. Yearly Vol. Illustrated. 9s.

Cathedral Churches of England and Wales. Descriptive, Historical, and Pictorial. With 150 Illustrations. 21s.

Changing Year, The. With Illustrations. 7s. 6d.

China Painting. By FLORENCE LEWIS. With Sixteen Coloured Plates, and a selection of Wood Engravings, with full Instructions. 5s.

Choice Dishes at Small Cost. By A. G. PAYNE. 3s. 6d. *Cheap Edition,* 1s.

Cities of the World: their Origin, Progress, and Present Aspect. Three Vols. Illustrated. 7s. 6d. each.

Civil Service, Guide to Employment in the. *New and Enlarged Edition.* 3s. 6d.

Civil Service. — Guide to Female Employment in Government Offices. Cloth, 1s.

Clinical Manuals for Practitioners and Students of Medicine. (*A List of Volumes forwarded post free on application to the Publishers.*)

Clothing, The Influence of, on Health. By FREDERICK TREVES, F.R.C.S. 2s.

Cobden Club, Works published for the:—

Writings of Richard Cobden. 6s.	The Trade Depression. 6d.
Local Government and Taxation in the United Kingdom. 5s.	Crown Colonies. 1s.
The Depression in the West Indies. 6d.	Our Land Laws of the Past. 3d.
The Three Panics. 1s.	Popular Fallacies Regarding Trade. 6d.
Free Trade versus Fair Trade. 1s. 6d.	Reciprocity Craze. 3d.
Pleas for Protection examined. 6d.	Western Farmer of America. 3d.
Free Trade and English Commerce. By A. Mongredien. 6d.	Transfer of Land by Registration. 6d.
	Reform of the English Land System. 3d.

Colonies and India, Our, How we Got Them, and Why we Keep Them. By Prof. C. RANSOME. 1s.

Columbus, Christopher, The Life and Voyages of. By WASHINGTON IRVING. Three Vols. 7s. 6d.

Cookery, Cassell's Dictionary of. Containing about Nine Thousand Recipes. 7s. 6d. ; Roxburgh, 10s. 6d.

Cookery, A Year's. By PHYLLIS BROWNE. Cloth gilt or oiled cloth, 3s. 6d.

Cook Book, Catherine Owen's New. 4s.

Co-operators, Working Men: What they have Done, and What they are Doing. By A. H. DYKE-ACLAND, M.P., and B. JONES.

Countries of the World, The. By ROBERT BROWN, M.A., Ph.D., &c. Complete in Six Vols., with about 750 Illustrations. 4to, 7s. 6d. each.

Cromwell, Oliver: The Man and his Mission. By J. ALLANSON PICTON, M.P. Cloth, 7s. 6d. ; morocco, cloth sides, 9s.

Cyclopædia, Cassell's Concise. With 12,000 subjects, brought down to the latest date. With about 600 Illustrations, 15s. ; Roxburgh, 18s.

Dairy Farming. By Prof. J. P. SHELDON. With 25 Fac-simile Coloured Plates, and numerous Wood Engravings. Cloth, 31s. 6d. ; half-morocco, 42s.

Decisive Events in History. By THOMAS ARCHER. With Sixteen Illustrations. Boards, 3s. 6d. ; cloth, 5s.

Decorative Design, Principles of. By CHRISTOPHER DRESSER, Ph.D. Illustrated. 5s.

Deserted Village Series, The. Consisting of *Éditions de luxe* of favourite poems by Standard Authors. Illustrated. Cloth gilt, 2s. 6d.; or Japanese morocco, 5s. each.

| Goldsmith's Deserted Village. | Wordsworth's Ode on Immortality, |
| Milton's L'Allegro and Il Pensoroso. | and Lines on Tintern Abbey. |

Songs from Shakespeare.

Dickens, Character Sketches from. SECOND and THIRD SERIES. With Six Original Drawings in each, by FREDERICK BARNARD. In Portfolio, 21s. each.

Diary of Two Parliaments. By H. W. LUCY. The Disraeli Parliament, 12s. The Gladstone Parliament, 12s.

Dog, The. By IDSTONE. Illustrated. 2s. 6d.

Dog, Illustrated Book of the. By VERO SHAW, B.A. With 28 Coloured Plates. Cloth bevelled, 35s. ; half-morocco, 45s.

Domestic Dictionary, The. An Encyclopædia for the Household. Cloth, 7s. 6d.

Doré's Adventures of Munchausen. Illustrated by GUSTAVE DORÉ. 5s.

Doré's Dante's Inferno. Illustrated by GUSTAVE DORÉ. *Popular Edition*, 21s.

Doré's Don Quixote. With about 400 Illustrations by DORÉ. 15s.

Doré's Fairy Tales Told Again. With 24 Full-page Engravings by DORÉ. 5s.

Doré Gallery, The. With 250 Illustrations by GUSTAVE DORÉ. 4to, 42s.

Doré's Milton's Paradise Lost. With Full-page Drawings by GUSTAVE DORÉ. 4to, 21s.

Edinburgh, Old and New, Cassell's. With 600 Illustrations. Three Vols., 9s. each ; library binding, £1 10s. the set.

Educational Year-Book, The. 6s.

Egypt: Descriptive, Historical, and Picturesque. By Prof. G. EBERS. Translated by CLARA BELL, with Notes by SAMUEL BIRCH, LL.D., &c. Two Vols. With 800 Original Engravings. Vol. I., £2 5s. ; Vol. II., £2 12s. 6d.

Electricity in the Service of Man. With nearly 850 Illustrations. 21s.

Electrician's Pocket-Book, The. By GORDON WIGAN, M.A. 5s.

Encyclopædic Dictionary, The. A New and Original Work of Reference to all the Words in the English Language. Ten Divisional Vols. now ready, 10s. 6d. each ; or the Double Divisional Vols., half-morocco, 21s. each.

Energy in Nature. By WM. LANT CARPENTER, B.Sc. 80 Illustrations. 3s. 6d.

England, Cassell's Illustrated History of. With 2,000 Illustrations. Ten Vols., 4to, 9s. each.

English History, The Dictionary of. Cloth, 21s. ; Roxburgh, 25s.

English Literature, Library of. By Prof. HENRY MORLEY. Complete in 5 vols., 7s. 6d. each.

    VOL. I.—SHORTER ENGLISH POEMS.
    VOL. II.—ILLUSTRATIONS OF ENGLISH RELIGION.
    VOL. III.—ENGLISH PLAYS.
    VOL. IV.—SHORTER WORKS IN ENGLISH PROSE.
    VOL. V. SKETCHES OF LONGER WORKS IN ENGLISH VERSE AND PROSE.
    Five Volumes handsomely bound in half-morocco, £5 5s.

English Literature, Morley's First Sketch. Revised Edition, 7s. 6d.
English Literature, The Dictionary of. By W. DAVENPORT ADAMS. *Cheap Edition.* 7s. 6d. ; Roxburgh, 10s. 6d.
English Literature, The Story of. By ANNA BUCKLAND. 5s.
English Poetesses. By ERIC S. ROBERTSON, M.A. 5s.
Æsop's Fables. With about 150 Illustrations by E. GRISET. Cloth, 7s. 6d. ; gilt edges, 10s. 6d.
Etching : Its Technical Processes, with Remarks on Collections and Collecting. By S. K. KOEHLER. Illustrated with 30 Full-page Plates. Price £4 4s.
Etiquette of Good Society. 1s. ; cloth, 1s. 6d.
Eye, Ear, and Throat, The Management of the. 3s. 6d.
Family Physician, The. By Eminent PHYSICIANS and SURGEONS. Cloth, 21s. ; half-morocco, 25s.
False Hopes. By Prof. GOLDWIN SMITH, M.A., LL.D., D.C.L. 6d.
Fenn, G. Manville, Works by. *Popular Editions.* Cloth boards, 2s. each.

Sweet Mace.   The Vicar's People.
Dutch the Diver; or, a Man's Mistake.   Cobweb's Father, and other Stories.
My Patients.   The Parson o' Dumford.
Poverty Corner.

Ferns, European. By JAMES BRITTEN, F.L.S. With 30 Fac-simile Coloured Plates by D. BLAIR, F.L.S. 21s.
Field Naturalist's Handbook, The. By the Rev. J. G. WOOD and THEODORE WOOD. 5s.
Figuier's Popular Scientific Works. With Several Hundred Illustrations in each. 3s. 6d. each.

The Human Race.   The Ocean World.
World Before the Deluge.   The Vegetable World.
Reptiles and Birds.   The Insect World.
Mammalia.

Figure Painting in Water Colours. With 16 Coloured Plates by BLANCHE MACARTHUR and JENNIE MOORE. With full Instructions. 7s. 6d.
Fine-Art Library, The. Edited by JOHN SPARKES, Principal of the South Kensington Art Schools. Each Book contains about 100 Illustrations. 5s. each.

Tapestry. By Eugène Müntz. Translated by Miss L. J. Davis.   The Education of the Artist. By Ernest Chesneau. Translated by Clara Bell. Non-Illustrated.
Engraving. By Le Vicomte Henri Delaborde. Translated by R. A. M. Stevenson.   Greek Archæology. By Maxime Collignon. Translated by Dr J. H. Wright.
The English School of Painting. By E. Chesneau. Translated by L. N. Etherington. With an Introduction by Prof. Ruskin.   Artistic Anatomy. By Prof. Duval. Translated by F. E. Fenton.
The Flemish School of Painting. By A. J. Wauters. Translated by Mrs. Henry Rossel.   The Dutch School of Painting. By Henry Havard. Translated by G. Powell.

Fisheries of the World, The. Illustrated. 4to, 9s.
Five Pound Note, The, and other Stories. By G. S. JEALOUS. 1s.
Flower Painting in Water Colours. First and Second Series. With 20 Fac-simile Coloured Plates in each by F. E. HULME, F.L.S., F.S.A. With Instructions by the Artist. Interleaved. 5s. each.
Flowers, and How to Paint Them. By MAUD NAFTEL. With Coloured Plates. 5s.
Forging of the Anchor, The. A Poem. By Sir SAMUEL FERGUSON, LL.D. With 20 Original Illustrations. Gilt edges, 5s. ; or Japanese morocco packed, 6s.
Fossil Reptiles, A History of British. By Sir RICHARD OWEN, K.C.B., F.R.S., &c. With 268 Plates. In Four Vols., £12 12s.
Four Years of Irish History (1845-49). By Sir GAVAN DUFFY, K.C.M.G. 21s.
Franco-German War, Cassell's History of. Two Vols. With 500 Illustrations. 9s. each.
Fresh-Water Fishes of Europe, The. By Prof. H. G. SEELEY, F.R.S. Cloth, 21s.
Garden Flowers, Familiar. FIRST, SECOND, THIRD, and FOURTH SERIES. By SHIRLEY HIBBERD. With 40 Full-page Coloured Plates in each. By F. E. HULME, F.L.S. Cloth gilt, 12s. 6d. each.
Gardening, Cassell's Popular. Illustrated. Complete in 4 Vols., 5s. each.

Gladstone, Life of the Rt. Hon. W. E. By BARNETT SMITH. With Portrait, 3s. 6d. *Jubilee Edition*, 1s.

Gleanings from Popular Authors. Two Vols. With Original Illustrations. 4to, 9s. each. Two Vols. in One, 15s.

Gold to Grey, From. Being Poems and Pictures of Life and Nature. By MARY D. BRINE. Illustrated. 7s. 6d.

Great Industries of Great Britain. With 400 Illustrations. 3 Vols., 7s. 6d. each.

Great Northern Railway, The Official Illustrated Guide to the. 1s.; or in cloth, 2s.

Great Painters of Christendom, The, from Cimabue to Wilkie. By JOHN FORBES-ROBERTSON. Illustrated throughout. *Popular Edition*, cloth gilt, 12s. 6d.

Great Western Railway, The Official Illustrated Guide to the. With Illustrations, 1s.; cloth, 2s.

Gulliver's Travels. With 88 Engravings by MORTEN. *Cheap Edition.* 5s.

Gun and its Development, The. By W. W. GREENER. Illustrated. 10s. 6d.

Health at School. By CLEMENT DUKES, M.D.B.S. 6s.

Health, The Book of. By Eminent Physicians and Surgeons. Cloth, 21s.; half-morocco, 25s.

Health, The Influence of Clothing on. By F. TREVES, F.R.C.S. 2s.

Heavens, The Story of the. By Sir ROBERT STAWELL BALL, LL.D., F.R.S., Royal Astronomer of Ireland. Coloured Plates and Wood Engravings. 31s. 6d.

Heroes of Britain in Peace and War. In Two Vols., with 300 Original Illustrations. Cloth, 5s. each. In one Vol., library binding, 10s. 6d.

Homes, Our, and How to Make them Healthy. By Eminent Authorities. Illustrated. 15s.; half-morocco, 21s.

Horse-Keeper, The Practical. By GEORGE FLEMING, LL.D., F.R.C.V.S. Illustrated. Crown 8vo, cloth, 7s. 6d.

Horse, the Book of the. By SAMUEL SIDNEY. With 25 *fac-simile* Coloured Plates. Demy 4to, 35s.; half-morocco, £2 5s.

Horses, the Simple Ailments of. By W. F. Illustrated. 5s.

Household Guide, Cassell's. With Illustrations and Coloured Plates. *New and Revised Edition*, complete in Four Vols., 20s.

How Women may Earn a Living. By MERCY GROGAN. 1s.

India, Cassell's History of. By JAMES GRANT. With 400 Illustrations. 15s.

India, the Coming Struggle for. By Prof. ARMINIUS VAMBÉRY. 5s.

India: the Land and the People. By Sir JAMES CAIRD, K.C.B. 10s. 6d.

In-door Amusements, Cards Games, and Fireside Fun, Cassell's. 2s. 6d.

Industrial Remuneration Conference. The Report of. 2s. 6d.

Insect Variety: its Propagation and Distribution. By A. H. SWINTON. 7s. 6d.

Invisible Life, Vignettes from. By J. BADCOCK, F.R.M.S. Illustrated. 3s. 6d.

Irish Parliament, The, What it Was, and What it Did. By J. G. SWIFT McNEILL, M.A. 1s.

Italy. By J. W. PROBYN. 7s. 6d.

Kennel Guide, Practical. By Dr. GORDON STABLES. Illustrated. 2s. 6d.

Kidnapped. By R. L. STEVENSON. 5s.

Khiva, A Ride to. By the late Col. FRED BURNABY. 1s. 6d.

Ladies' Physician, The. By a London Physician. 6s.

Land Question, The. By Prof. J. ELLIOT, M.R.A.C. 10s. 6d.

Landscape Painting in Oils, A Course of Lessons in. By A. F. GRACE. With Nine Reproductions in Colour. *Cheap Edition*, 25s.

Law, About Going to. By A. J. WILLIAMS, M.P. 2s. 6d.

Letts's Diaries and other Time-saving Publications are now published exclusively by CASSELL & COMPANY. (*A list sent post free on application.*)

Liberal, Why I am a. By ANDREW REID. 2s. 6d. *People's Edition*, 1s.

London & North-Western Railway Official Illustrated Guide. 1s.; cloth, 2s.
London, Greater. By EDWARD WALFORD. Two Vols. With about 400 Illustrations. 9s. each.
London, Old and New. By WALTER THORNBURY and EDWARD WALFORD. Six Vols., each containing about 200 Illustrations and Maps. Cloth, 9s. each.
London's Roll of Fame. With Portraits and Illustrations. 12s. 6d.
Longfellow, H. W., Choice Poems by. Illustrated by his Son, ERNEST W. LONGFELLOW. 6s.
Longfellow's Poetical Works. Illustrated. *Popular Edition,* 16s.
Love's Extremes, At. By MAURICE THOMPSON. 5s.
Luther, Martin: The Man and his Work. By Dr. PETER BAYNE. Two Vols. 24s.
Mechanics, The Practical Dictionary of. Containing 15,000 Drawings. Four Vols. 21s. each.
Medicine, Manuals for Students of. (*A List forwarded post free on application.*)
· **Midland Railway, The Official Illustrated Guide to the.** 1s.; cloth, 2s.
Modern Artists, Some. With highly-finished Engravings. 12s. 6d.
Modern Europe, A History of. By C. A. FYFFE, M.A. Vol. I. From 1792 to 1814. 12s. Vol. II. From 1814 to 1848. 12s.
Music, Illustrated History of. By EMIL NAUMANN. Edited by the Rev. Sir F. A. GORE OUSELEY, Bart. Illustrated. Two Vols. 31s. 6d.
National Library, Cassell's. In Weekly Volumes, each containing about 192 pages. Paper covers, 3d.; cloth, 6d. (*A List sent post free on application.*)
Natural History, Cassell's Concise. By E. PERCEVAL WRIGHT, M.A., M.D., F.L.S. With several Hundred Illustrations. 7s. 6d. Roxburgh, 10s. 6d.
Natural History, Cassell's New. Edited by Prof. P. MARTIN DUNCAN, M.B., F.R.S., F.G.S. With Contributions by Eminent Scientific Writers. Complete in Six Vols. With about 2,000 high-class Illustrations. Extra crown 4to, cloth, 9s. each.
Nature, Short Studies from. Illustrated. 5s.
Neutral Tint, A Course of Painting in. With Twenty-four Plates by R. P. LEITCH. With full Instructions to the Pupil. 5s.
Nimrod in the North; or, Hunting and Fishing Adventures in the Arctic Regions. By FREDERICK SCHWATKA. Illustrated, 7s. 6d.
Nursing for the Home and for the Hospital, A Handbook of. By CATHERINE J. WOOD. *Cheap Edition.* 1s. 6d.; cloth, 2s.
Oil Painting, A Manual of. By Hon. JOHN COLLIER. Cloth, 2s. 6d.
On the Equator. By H. DE W. Illustrated with Photos. 3s. 6d.
Our Own Country. Six Vols. With 1,200 Illustrations. Cloth, 7s. 6d. each.
Outdoor Sports and Indoor Amusements. With nearly 1,000 Illustrations. 9s.
Paris, Cassell's Illustrated Guide to. 1s.; cloth, 2s.
Parliaments, A Diary of Two. By H. W. LUCY. The Disraeli Parliament, 1874—1880. 12s. The Gladstone Parliament. 12s.
Paxton's Flower Garden. By Sir JOSEPH PAXTON and Prof. LINDLEY. Revised by THOMAS BAINES, F.R.H.S. Three Vols. With 100 Coloured Plates. £1 1s. each.
Peoples of the World, The. By Dr. ROBERT BROWN. Vols. I. to V. now ready. With Illustrations. 7s. 6d. each.
Perak and the Malays. By Major FRED MCNAIR. Illustrated. 10s. 6d.
Phantom City, The. By W. WESTALL. 5s.
Photography for Amateurs. By T. C. HEPWORTH. Illustrated, 1s.; or cloth, 1s. 6d.
Phrase and Fable, Dictionary of. By the Rev. Dr. BREWER. *Cheap Edition,* *Enlarged,* cloth, 3s. 6d.; or with leather back, 4s. 6d.
Picturesque America. Complete in Four Vols., with 48 Exquisite Steel Plates, and about 800 Original Wood Engravings. £2 2s. each.
Picturesque Canada. With about 600 Original Illustrations. Two Vols., £3 3s. each.

Picturesque Europe. Complete in Five Vols. Each containing 13 Exquisite Steel Plates, from Original Drawings, and nearly 200 Original Illustrations. £10 10s. ; half-morocco, £15 15s. ; morocco gilt, £26 5s. The POPULAR EDITION is published in Five Vols., 18s. each, of which Four Vols. are now ready.

Pigeon Keeper, The Practical. By LEWIS WRIGHT. Illustrated. 3s. 6d.

Pigeons, The Book of. By ROBERT FULTON. Edited by LEWIS WRIGHT. With 50 Coloured Plates and numerous Wood Engravings. 31s. 6d. ; half-morocco, £2 2s.

Poems and Pictures. With numerous Illustrations. 5s.

Poems, Representative of Living Poets, American and English. Selected by the Poets themselves. 15s.

Poets, Cassell's Miniature Library of the :—

Burns. Two Vols. 2s. 6d.	**Milton.** Two Vols. 2s. 6d.
Byron. Two Vols. 2s. 6d.	**Scott.** Two Vols. 2s. 6d.
Hood. Two Vols. 2s. 6d.	**Sheridan and Goldsmith.** 2 Vols. 2s. 6d
Longfellow. Two Vols. 2s. 6d.	**Wordsworth.** Two Vols. 2s. 6d.

Shakespeare. Twelve Vols., in box, 15s.

Police Code, and Manual of the Criminal Law. By C. E. HOWARD VINCENT, M.P., late Director of Criminal Investigations. 2s.

Popular Library, Cassell's. A Series of New and Original Works. Cloth, 1s. each.

The Russian Empire.	Domestic Folk Lore.
The Religious Revolution in the Six-	The Rev. Rowland Hill: Preacher and
teenth Century.	Wit.
English Journalism.	Boswell and Johnson: their Companions
The Huguenots.	and Contemporaries.
Our Colonial Empire.	The Scottish Covenanters.
The Young Man in the Battle of Life.	History of the Free-Trade Movement in
John Wesley.	England.
The Story of the English Jacobins.	

Poultry Keeper, The Practical. By L. WRIGHT. With Coloured Plates and Illustrations. 3s. 6d.

Poultry, The Book of. By LEWIS WRIGHT. *Popular Edition.* With Illustrations on Wood, 10s. 6d.

Poultry, The Illustrated Book of. By L. WRIGHT. With Fifty Exquisite Coloured Plates, and numerous Wood Engravings. Cloth, 31s. 6d. ; half-morocco, £2 2s.

Rabbit-Keeper, The Practical. By CUNICULUS. Illustrated. 3s. 6d.

Rainbow Series, Cassell's. Consisting of New and Original Works of Romance and Adventure by Leading Writers. 192 pages, crown 8vo, price 1s. each.

As it was Written. By S. LUSKA.	A Crimson Stain. By A BRADSHAW.
Morgan's Horror. By C. MANVILLE FENN.	

Rays from the Realms of Nature. By the Rev. J. NEIL, M.A. Illustrated. 2s. 6d.

Red Library of English and American Classics, The. Stiff covers, 1s. each ; cloth, 2s. each ; or half-calf, marbled edges, 5s. each.

Edgar Allan Poe.	Yellowplush Papers.
Prose and Poetry, Selections from.	Handy Andy.
Old Mortality.	Selected Plays.
The Hour and the Man.	American Humour.
Washington Irving's Sketch-Book.	Sketches by Boz.
Last Days of Palmyra.	Macaulay's Lays and Selected Essays.
Tales of the Borders.	Harry Lorrequer.
Pride and Prejudice.	Old Curiosity Shop.
Last of the Mohicans.	Rienzi.
Heart of Midlothian.	The Talisman.
Last Days of Pompeii.	Pickwick (Two Vols.)

Scarlet Letter.

Royal River, The : The Thames, from Source to Sea. With Descriptive Text and a Series of beautiful Engravings. £2 2s.

Russia. By D. MACKENZIE WALLACE, M.A. 5s.

Russo-Turkish War, Cassell's History of. With about 500 Illustrations. Two Vols., 9s. each ; library binding, One Vol., 15s.

Sandwith, Humphry. A Memoir by his Nephew, T. HUMPHRY WARD. 7s. 6d.

Saturday Journal, Cassell's. Yearly Volume. 6s.

Science for All. Edited by Dr. ROBERT BROWN, M.A., F.L.S., &c. With 1,500 Illustrations. Five Vols., 9s. each.

Sea, The: Its Stirring Story of Adventure, Peril, and Heroism. By F. WHYMPER. With 400 Illustrations. Four Vols., 7s. 6d. each.

Sent Back by the Angels. And other Ballads of Home and Homely Life. By FREDERICK LANGBRIDGE, M.A. 4s. 6d.

Sepia Painting, A Course of. Two Vols., with Twelve Coloured Plates in each, and numerous Engravings. Each, 3s.

Shaftesbury, The Earl of, K.G., The Life and Work of. By EDWIN HODDER. With Portraits. Three Vols. 36s.

Shakespeare's Romeo and Juliet. *Édition de Luxe.* Illustrated with Twelve Superb Photogravures from Original Drawings by F. DICKSEE, A.R.A. £5 5s.

Shakspere, The Leopold. With 400 Illustrations, and an Introduction by F. J. FURNIVALL. Small 4to, cloth, 6s.; cloth gilt, 7s. 6d.; half-morocco, 10s. 6d.; full morocco, £1 1s.

Shakspere, The Royal. With Exquisite Steel Plates and Wood Engravings. Three Vols. 15s. each.

Shakespeare, Cassell's Quarto Edition. Edited by CHARLES and MARY COWDEN CLARKE, and containing about 600 Illustrations by H. C. SELOUS. Complete in Three Vols., cloth gilt, £3 3s.—Also published in Three separate Volumes, in cloth, viz.:—The COMEDIES, 21s.; The HISTORICAL PLAYS, 18s. 6d.; The TRAGEDIES, 25s.

Shakespearean Scenes and Characters. Illustrative of Thirty Plays of Shakespeare. With Thirty Steel Plates and Ten Wood Engravings. The Text written by AUSTIN BRERETON. Royal 4to, 21s.

Sketching from Nature in Water Colours. By AARON PENLEY. With Illustrations in Chromo-Lithography. 15s.

Skin and Hair, The Management of the. By MALCOLM MORRIS, F.R.C.S. 2s.

Smith, The Adventures and Discourses of Captain John. By JOHN ASHTON. Illustrated. 5s.

Sports and Pastimes, Cassell's Book of. With more than 800 Illustrations and Coloured Frontispiece. 768 pages, 7s. 6d.

Steam Engine, The Theory and Action of the: for Practical Men. By W. H. NORTHCOTT, C.E. 3s. 6d.

Stock Exchange Year-Book, The. By THOMAS SKINNER. 10s. 6d.

Stones of London, The. By E. F. FLOWER. 6d.

"Stories from Cassell's." 6d. each; cloth lettered, 9d. each.

My Aunt's Match-making.	"Running Pilot."
Told by her Sister.	The Mortgage Money.
The Silver Look.	Gourlay Brothers.

A Great Mistake.

. The above are also issued, Three Volumes in One, cloth, price 2s. each.

Sunlight and Shade. With numerous Exquisite Engravings. 7s. 6d.

Surgery, Memorials of the Craft of, in England. With an Introduction by Sir JAMES PAGET. 21s.

Telegraph Guide, The. Illustrated. 1s.

Thackeray, Character Sketches from. Six New and Original Drawings by FREDERICK BARNARD, reproduced in Photogravure. 21s.

Three and Sixpenny Library of Standard Tales, &c. All Illustrated and bound in cloth gilt. Crown 8vo, 3s. 6d. each.

Jane Austen and her Works.	In Duty Bound.
Better than Good.	The Half Sisters.
Mission Life in Greece and Palestine.	Peggy Oglivie's Inheritance.
The Dingy House at Kensington.	The Family Honour.
The Romance of Trade.	Esther West.
The Three Homes.	Working to Win.
My Guardian.	Krilof and his Fables. By W. R. S
School Girls.	Ralston, M.A.
Deepdale Vicarage.	Fairy Tales. By Prof. Morley.

Heroines of the Mission Field.

Tot Book for all Public Examinations. By W. S. THOMSON, M.A. 1s.

Trajan. An American Novel. By H. F. KEENAN. 7s. 6d.

Transformations of Insects, The. By Prof. P. MARTIN DUNCAN, M.B., F.R.S. With 240 Illustrations. 6s.

Treasure Island. By R. L. STEVENSON. Illustrated. 5s.

Treatment, The Year-Book of. A Critical Review for Practitioners of Medicine and Surgery. 5s.

Tree Painting in Water Colours. By W. H. J. BOOT. With Eighteen
Coloured Plates, and valuable instructions by the Artist. 5s.

Trees, Familiar. By G. S. BOULGER, F.L.S. With Forty Coloured Plates by
W. H. J. BOOT. First Series. 12s. 6d.

Twenty Photogravures of Pictures in the Salon of 1885, by the leading
French Artists. In Portfolio. Only a limited number of copies have been produced,
terms for which can be obtained of all Booksellers.

"Unicode": The Universal Telegraphic Phrase Book. 2s. 6d.

United States, Cassell's History of the. By EDMUND OLLIER. With 600
Illustrations. Three Vols., 9s. each.

Universal History, Cassell's Illustrated. With nearly ONE THOUSAND
ILLUSTRATIONS. Vol. I. Early and Greek History.—Vol. II. The Roman Period.—
Vol. III. The Middle Ages.—Vol. IV. Modern History. 9s. each.

Vicar of Wakefield and other Works by OLIVER GOLDSMITH. Illustrated. 3s. 6d.

Water-Colour Painting, A Course of. With Twenty-four Coloured Plates by
R. P. LEITCH, and full Instructions to the Pupil. 5s.

Wealth Creation. By A. MONGREDIEN. 5s.

Westall, W., Novels by. *Popular Editions.* Cloth, 2s. each.

The Old Factory.	Red Ryvington.
Ralph Norbreck's Trust.	

What Girls Can Do. By PHYLLIS BROWNE. 2s. 6d.

Wild Animals and Birds: their Haunts and Habits. By Dr. ANDREW
WILSON. Illustrated. 7s. 6d.

Wild Birds, Familiar. First and Second Series. By W. SWAYSLAND. With 40
Coloured Plates in each. 12s. 6d. each.

Wild Flowers, Familiar. By F. E. HULME, F.L.S., F.S.A. Five Series. With
40 Coloured Plates in each. 12s. 6d. each.

Winter in India, A. By the Rt. Hon. W. E. BAXTER, M.P. 5s.

Wise Woman, The. By GEORGE MACDONALD. 2s. 6d.

Wood Magic: A Fable. By RICHARD JEFFERIES. 6s.

World of the Sea. Translated from the French of MOQUIN TANDON, by the
Very Rev. H. MARTYN HART, M.A. Illustrated. Cloth. 6s.

World of Wit and Humour, The. With 400 Illustrations. Cloth, 7s. 6d. ; cloth
gilt, gilt edges, 10s. 6d.

World of Wonders, The. Two Vols. With 400 Illustrations. 7s. 6d. each.

Yule Tide. CASSELL'S CHRISTMAS ANNUAL. 1s.

MAGAZINES.

The Quiver, for Sunday Reading. Monthly, 6d.

Cassell's Family Magazine. Monthly, 7d.

"Little Folks" Magazine. Monthly, 6d.

The Magazine of Art. Monthly, 1s.

Cassell's Saturday Journal. Weekly, 1d. ; Monthly, 6d.

₊ *Full particulars of CASSELL & COMPANY'S Monthly Serial
Publications, numbering upwards of* 50 *Works, will be found in*
CASSELL & COMPANY's COMPLETE CATALOGUE, *sent post free on*
application.

Catalogues of CASSELL & COMPANY'S PUBLICATIONS, which may be had at all
Booksellers', or will be sent post free on application to the Publishers :—
CASSELL'S COMPLETE CATALOGUE, containing particulars of One Thousand
Volumes.
CASSELL'S CLASSIFIED CATALOGUE, in which their Works are arranged according
to price, from *Threepence to Twenty-five Guineas.*
CASSELL'S EDUCATIONAL CATALOGUE, containing particulars of CASSELL &
COMPANY'S Educational Works and Students' Manuals.

CASSELL & COMPANY, LIMITED, *Ludgate Hill, London.*

Bibles and Religious Works.

Bible, The Crown Illustrated. With about 1,000 Original Illustrations. With References, &c. 1,248 pages, crown 4to, cloth, 7s. 6d.

Bible, Cassell's Illustrated Family. With 900 Illustrations. Leather, gilt edges, £2 10s. ; full morocco, £3 10s.

Bible Dictionary, Cassell's. With nearly 600 Illustrations. 7s. 6d.

Bible Educator, The. Edited by the Very Rev. Dean PLUMPTRE, D.D. With Illustrations, Maps, &c. Four Vols., cloth, 6s. each.

Bible Work at Home and Abroad. Yearly Volume, 3s. 6d.

Bunyan's Pilgrim's Progress (Cassell's Illustrated). Demy 4to. Illustrated throughout. 7s. 6d.

Bunyan's Pilgrim's Progress. With Illustrations. *Popular Edition*, 3s. 6d.

Child's Life of Christ, The. Complete in One Handsome Volume, with about 200 Original Illustrations. Demy 4to, gilt edges, 21s.

Child's Bible, The. With 200 Illustrations. Demy 4to, 830 pp. 143*rd Thousand.* *Cheap Edition*, 7s. 6d.

Church at Home, The. A Series of Short Sermons. By the Rt. Rev. ROWLEY HILL, D.D., Bishop of Sodor and Man. 5s.

Commentary, The New Testament, for English Readers. Edited by the Rt. Rev. C. J. ELLICOTT, D.D., Lord Bishop of Gloucester and Bristol. In Three Volumes, 21s. each.
Vol. I.—The Four Gospels.
Vol. II.—The Acts, Romans, Corinthians, Galatians.
Vol. III.—The remaining Books of the New Testament.

Commentary, The Old Testament, for English Readers. Edited by the Rt. Rev. C. J. ELLICOTT, D.D., Lord Bishop of Gloucester and Bristol. Complete in 5 Vols., 21s. each.

Vol. I.—Genesis to Numbers.	Vol. III.—Kings I. to Esther.
Vol. II.—Deuteronomy to Samuel II.	Vol. IV.—Job to Isaiah.

Vol. V.—Jeremiah to Malachi.

Day-Dawn in Dark Places; or Wanderings and Work in Bechwanaland, South Africa. By the Rev. JOHN MACKENZIE. Illustrated throughout. 3s. 6d.

Difficulties of Belief, Some. By the Rev. T. TEIGNMOUTH SHORE, M.A. *New and Cheap Edition.* 2s. 6d.

Doré Bible. With 230 Illustrations by GUSTAVE DORÉ. 2 Vols., cloth, £2 10s. ; Persian morocco, £3 10s. ; Original Edition, 2 Vols., cloth, £8.

Early Days of Christianity, The. By the Ven. Archdeacon FARRAR, D.D., F.R.S.
LIBRARY EDITION. Two Vols., 24s. ; morocco, £2 2s.
POPULAR EDITION. Complete in One Volume, cloth, 6s. ; cloth, gilt edges, 7s. 6d. ; Persian morocco, 10s. 6d. ; tree-calf, 15s.

Family Prayer-Book, The. Edited by Rev. Canon GARBETT, M.A., and Rev. S. MARTIN. Extra crown 4to, cloth, 5s. ; morocco, 18s.

Geikie, Cunningham, D.D., Works by :—

Hours with the Bible. Six Vols. 6s. each.	Old Testament Characters. 6s.
Entering on Life. 3s. 6d.	The Life and Words of Christ. Two Vols.,
The Precious Promises. 2s. 6d.	cloth, 30s. Students' Edition, Two Vols.,
The English Reformation. 5s.	16s.

Glories of the Man of Sorrows, The. Sermons preached at St. James's, Piccadilly. By the Rev. H. G. BONAVIA HUNT. 2s. 6d.

Gospel of Grace, The. By a LINDESIE. Cloth, 3s. 6d.

Helps to Belief. A Series of Helpful Manuals on the Religions Difficulties of the Day. Edited by the Rev. TEIGNMOUTH SHORE, M.A., Chaplain in Ordinary to the Queen. Cloth, 1s. each.

CREATION. By the Lord Bishop of Carlisle.	THE MORALITY OF THE OLD TESTAMENT. By the Rev. Newman Smyth, D.D.
MIRACLES. By the Rev. Brownlow Maitland, M.A.	
PRAYER. By the Rev. T. Teignmouth Shore, M.A.	THE DIVINITY OF OUR LORD. By the Lord Bishop of Derry.

In Preparation.

THE RESURRECTION. By the Lord Archbishop of York.	THE ATONEMENT. By the Lord Bishop of Peterborough.

"Heart Chords." A Series of Works by Eminent Divines. Bound in cloth, red edges, 1s. each.

My Father. By the Right Rev. Ashton Oxenden, late Bishop of Montreal.
My Bible. By the Rt. Rev. W. Boyd Carpenter, Bishop of Ripon.
My Work for God. By the Right Rev. Bishop Cotterill.
My Object in Life. By the Ven. Archdeacon Farrar, D.D.
My Aspirations. By the Rev. G. Matheson, D.D.
My Emotional Life. By the Rev. Preb. Chadwick, D.D.
My Body. By the Rev. Prof. W. G. Blaikie, D.D.

My Soul. By the Rev. P. B. Power, M.A.
My Growth in Divine Life. By the Rev. Prebendary Reynolds, M.A.
My Hereafter. By the Very Rev. Dean Bickersteth.
My Walk with God. By the Very Rev. Dean Montgomery.
My Aids to the Divine Life. By the Very Rev. Dean Boyle.
My Sources of Strength. By the Rev. E. E. Jenkins, M.A., Secretary of the Wesleyan Missionary Society.

Life of Christ, The. By the Ven. Archdeacon FARRAR, D.D., F.R.S., Chaplain in Ordinary to the Queen.

> ILLUSTRATED EDITION, with about 300 Original Illustrations. Extra crown 4to, cloth, gilt edges, 21s. ; morocco antique, 42s.
> LIBRARY EDITION. Two Vols. Cloth, 24s. ; morocco, 42s.
> BIJOU EDITION. Five Volumes, in box, 10s. 6d. the set.
> POPULAR EDITION, in One Vol. 8vo, cloth, 6s. ; cloth, gilt edges, 7s. 6d. ; Persian morocco, gilt edges, 10s. 6d. ; tree-calf, 15s.

Marriage Ring, The. By WILLIAM LANDELS, D.D. Bound in white leatherette, gilt edges, in box, 6s. ; morocco, 8s. 6d.

Moses and Geology; or, The Harmony of the Bible with Science. By SAMUEL KINNS, Ph.D., F.R.A.S. Illustrated. *Cheap Edition.* 6s.

Music of the Bible, The. By J. STAINER, M.A., Mus. Doc. 2s. 6d.

Patriarchs, The. By the late Rev. W. HANNA, D.D., and the Ven. Archdeacon NORRIS, B.D. 2s. 6d.

Protestantism, The History of. By the Rev. J. A. WYLIE, LL.D. Containing upwards of 600 Original Illustrations. Three Vols., 27s. ; Library Edition, 30s.

Quiver Yearly Volume, The. With 250 high-class Illustrations. 7s. 6d. Also Monthly, 6d.

Revised Version—Commentary on the Revised Version of the New Testament. By the Rev. W. G. HUMPHRY, D.D. 7s. 6d.

Sacred Poems, The Book of. Edited by the Rev. Canon BAYNES, M.A. With Illustrations. Cloth, gilt edges, 5s.

St. George for England; and other Sermons preached to Children. By the Rev. T. TEIGNMOUTH SHORE, M.A. 5s.

St. Paul, The Life and Work of. By the Ven. Archdeacon FARRAR, D.D., F.R.S., Chaplain in Ordinary to the Queen.

> LIBRARY EDITION. Two Vols., cloth, 24s. ; morocco, 42s.
> ILLUSTRATED EDITION, complete in One Volume, with about 300 Illustrations, £1 1s. : morocco, £2 2s.
> POPULAR EDITION. One Volume, 8vo, cloth, 6s. ; cloth, gilt edges, 7s. 6d. ; Persian morocco, 10s. 6d. ; tree-calf, 15s.

Secular Life, The Gospel of the. Sermons preached at Oxford. By the Hon. W. H. FREMANTLE, Canon of Canterbury. 5s.

Sermons Preached at Westminster Abbey. By ALFRED BARRY, D.D., D.C.L., Primate of Australia. 5s.

Shall We Know One Another? By the Rt. Rev. J. C. RYLE, D.D., Bishop of Liverpool. *New and Enlarged Edition.* Cloth limp, 1s.

Simon Peter: His Life, Times, and Friends. By E. HODDER. 5s.

Twilight of Life, The. Words of Counsel and Comfort for the Aged. By JOHN ELLERTON, M.A. 1s. 6d.

Voice of Time, The. By JOHN STROUD. Cloth gilt, 1s.

Educational Works and Students' Manuals.

Alphabet, Cassell's Pictorial. Size, 35 inches by 42½ inches. Mounted on Linen, with rollers. 3s. 6d.

Algebra, The Elements of. By Prof. WALLACE, M.A., 1s.

Arithmetics, The Modern School. By GEORGE RICKS, B.Sc. Lond. With Test Cards. (*List on application.*)

Book-Keeping. By THEODORE JONES. FOR SCHOOLS, 2s.; or cloth, 3s. FOR THE MILLION, 2s.; or cloth, 3s. Books for Jones's System. Ruled Sets of, 2s.

Chemistry, The Public School. By J. H. ANDERSON, M.A. 2s. 6d.

Commentary, The New Testament. Edited by Bishop ELLICOTT. Handy Volume Edition. Suitable for School and general use.

St. Matthew. 3s. 6d.	Romans. 2s. 6d.	Titus, Philemon, Hebrews,
St. Mark. 3s.	Corinthians I. and II. 3s.	and James. 3s.
St. Luke. 3s. 6d.	Galatians, Ephesians, and	Peter, Jude, and John. 3s.
St. John. 3s. 6d.	Philippians. 3s.	The Revelation. 3s.
The Acts of the Apostles. 3s. 6d.	Colossians, Thessalonians, and Timothy. 3s.	An Introduction to the New Testament. 2s. 6d.

Commentary, Old Testament. Edited by Bishop ELLICOTT. Handy Volume Edition. Suitable for School and general use.

Genesis. 3s. 6d.	Leviticus. 3s.	Deuteronomy. 2s. 6d.
Exodus. 3s.	Numbers. 2s. 6d.	

Copy-Books, Cassell's Graduated. Complete in 16 Books. 2d. each.

Copy-Books. The Modern School. Complete in 12 Books. 2d. each.

Drawing Books for Young Artists. 4 Books. 6d. each.

Drawing Books, Superior. 3 Books. Printed in Fac-simile by Lithography, price 5s. each.

Drawing Copies, Cassell's Modern School Freehand. First Grade, 1s.; Second Grade, 2s.

Drawing Copies, Cassell's Standard. In 7 Books. Price 2d. each.

Electricity, Practical. By Prof. W. E. AYRTON. Illustrated. 5s.

Energy and Motion: A Text-Book of Elementary Mechanics. By WILLIAM PAICE, M.A. Illustrated. 1s. 6d.

English Literature, A First Sketch of, from the Earliest Period to the Present Time. By Prof. HENRY MORLEY. 7s. 6d.

Euclid, Cassell's. Edited by Prof. WALLACE, M.A. 1s.

Euclid, The First Four Books of. In paper, 6d.; cloth, 9d.

French Reader, Cassell's Public School. By GUILLAUME S. CONRAD. 2s. 6d.

French, Cassell's Lessons in. *New and Revised Edition.* Parts 1. and 11., each 2s. 6d.; complete, 4s. 6d. Key, 1s. 6d.

French-English and English-French Dictionary. *Entirely New and Enlarged Edition.* 1,150 pages, 8vo, cloth, 3s. 6d.

Galbraith and Haughton's Scientific Manuals. By the Rev. Prof. GALBRAITH, M.A., and the Rev. Prof. HAUGHTON, M.D., D.C.L.

Arithmetic. 3s. 6d.	Optics. 2s. 6d.
Plane Trigonometry. 2s. 6d.	Hydrostatics. 3s. 6d.
Euclid. Books I., II., III. 2s. 6d. Books IV., V., VI. 2s. 6d.	Astronomy. 5s.
Mathematical Tables. 3s. 6d.	Steam Engine. 3s. 6d.
Mechanics. 3s. 6d.	Algebra. Part I., cloth, 2s. 6d. Complete, 7s. 6d.
	Tides and Tidal Currents, with Tidal Cards, 3s.

German of To-day. By Dr. HEINEMANN. 1s. 6d.

German-English and English-German Dictionary. 3s. 5d.

German Reading, First Lessons in. By A. JAGST. Illustrated. 1s.

Handbook of New Code of Regulations. By JOHN F. MOSS. 1s.; cloth, 2s.

Historical Course for Schools, Cassell's. Illustrated throughout. I.—Stories from English History, 1s. 11.—The Simple Outline of English History, 1s. 3d. III.—The Class History of England, 2s. 6d.

Latin-English and English-Latin Dictionary. By J. R. BEARD, D.D., and C. BEARD, B.A. Crown 8vo, 914 pp., 3s. 6d.

Little Folks' History of England. By ISA CRAIG-KNOX. With 30 Illustrations. 1s. 6d.

Making of the Home, The : A Book of Domestic Economy for School and Home Use. By Mrs. SAMUEL A. BARNETT. 1s. 6d.

Marlborough Books.

Arithmetic Examples. 3s.	French Exercises. 3s. 6d.
Arithmetic Rules. 1s. 6d.	French Grammar. 2s. 6d.

German Grammar. 3s. 6d.

Music, An Elementary Manual of. By HENRY LESLIE. 1s.

Natural Philosophy. By Rev. Prof. HAUGHTON, F.R.S. Illustrated. 3s. 6d.

Popular Educator, Cassell's. *New and Thoroughly Revised Edition.* Illustrated throughout. Complete in Six Vols., 5s. each ; or in Three Vols., half calf, 42s. the set.

Physical Science, Intermediate Text-Book of. By F. H. BOWMAN, D.Sc., F.R.A.S., F.L.S. Illustrated. 3s. 6d.

Readers, Cassell's Readable. Carefully graduated, extremely interesting, and illustrated throughout. *(List on application.)*

Readers, Cassell's Historical. Illustrated throughout, printed on superior paper, and strongly bound in cloth. *(List on application.)*

Readers for Infant Schools, Coloured. Three Books. Each containing 48 pages, including 8 pages in colours. 4d. each.

Reader, The Citizen. By H. O. ARNOLD-FORSTER. With Preface by the late Rt. Hon. W. E. FORSTER, M.P. 1s. 6d.

Readers, The Modern Geographical. Illustrated throughout, and strongly bound in cloth. *(List on application.)*

Readers, The Modern School. Illustrated. *(List on application.)*

Reading and Spelling Book, Cassell's Illustrated. 1s.

Right Lines ; or, Form and Colour. With Illustrations. 1s.

School Manager's Manual. By F. C. MILLS, M.A. 1s.

Shakspere Reading Book, The. By H. COURTHOPE BOWEN, M.A. Illustrated. 3s. 6d. Also issued in Three Books, 1s. each.

Shakspere's Plays for School Use. 5 Books. Illustrated. 6d. each.

Spelling, A Complete Manual of. By J. D. MORELL, LL.D. 1s.

Technical Manuals, Cassell's. Illustrated throughout :—

Handrailing and Staircasing. 3s. 6d.	Machinists & Engineers, Drawing for. 4s. 6d.
Bricklayers, Drawing for. 3s.	Model Drawing. 3s.
Building Construction. 2s.	Orthographical and Isometrical Projection. 2s.
Cabinet-Makers, Drawing for. 3s.	
Carpenters & Joiners, Drawing for. 3s. 6d.	Practical Perspective. 3s.
Gothic Stonework. 3s.	Stonemasons, Drawing for. 3s.
Linear Drawing & Practical Geometry. 2s.	Applied Mechanics. By Sir R. S. Ball, LL.D. 2s.
Linear Drawing and Projection. The Two Vols. in One, 3s. 6d.	Systematic Drawing and Shading. By Charles Ryan. 2s.
Metal-Plate Workers, Drawing for. 3s.	

Technical Educator, Cassell's. Illustrated throughout. Popular Edition. Four Vols., 5s. each.

Technology, Manuals of. Edited by Prof. AYRTON, F.R.S., and RICHARD WORMELL, D.Sc., M.A. Illustrated throughout.

The Dyeing of Textile Fabrics. By Prof. Hummel. 5s.	Design in Textile Fabrics. By T. R. Ashenhurst. 4s. 6d.
Watch and Clock Making. By D. Glasgow. 4s. 6d.	Practical Mechanics. By Prof. Perry, M.E. 3s. 6d.
Steel and Iron. By W. H. Greenwood, F.C.S. Assoc. M.I.C.E., &c., 5s.	Cutting Tools Worked by Hand and Machine. By Prof. Smith. 3s. 6d.
Spinning Woollen and Worsted. By W. S. Bright McLaren. 4s. 6d.	Practical Electricity. By Prof. W. E. Ayrton. Illustrated. 9s.

Other Volumes in preparation. A Prospectus sent post free on application.

Books for Young People.

Under Bayard's Banner. By HENRY FRITH. Illustrated. 5s.

The King's Command. A Story for Girls. By MAGGIE SYMINGTON. Illustrated. 5s.

The Romance of Invention. By JAMES BURNLEY. Illustrated. 5s.

The Tales of the Sixty Mandarins. By P. V. RAMASWAMI RAJU. With an Introduction by Prof. HENRY MORLEY. Illustrated. 5s.

A World of Girls: A Story of a School. By L. T. MEADE. Illustrated. 3s. 6d.

Lost among White Africans: A Boy's Adventures on the Upper Congo. By DAVID KER. Illustrated. 3s. 6d.

Perils Afloat and Brigands Ashore. By ALFRED ELWES. Illustrated. 3s. 6d.

Freedom's Sword: A Story of the Days of Wallace and Bruce. By ANNIE S. SWAN. Illustrated. 3s. 6d.

Strong to Suffer: A Story of the Jews. By E. WYNNE. Illustrated. 2s. 6d.

The Merry-go-Round. Poems for Children. Illustrated throughout. 5s.

Heroes of the Indian Empire; or, Stories of Valour and Victory. By ERNEST FOSTER. Illustrated. 2s. 6d.

In Letters of Flame: A Story of the Waldenses. By C. L. MATÉAUX. Illustrated. 2s. 6d.

Through Trial to Triumph. By MADELINE B. HUNT. Illustrated. 2s. 6d.

Sunday School Reward Books. By Popular Authors. With Four Original Illustrations in each. Cloth gilt, 1s. 6d. each.

Rhoda's Reward; or, "If Wishes were Horses."

Jack Marston's Anchor.

Frank's Life-Battle; or, The Three Friends.

Rags and Rainbows: a Story of Thanksgiving.

Uncle William's Charge; or, The Broken Trust.

Pretty Pink's Purpose; or, Two Little Street Merchants.

"Golden Mottoes" Series, The. Each Book containing 208 pages, with Four full-page Original Illustrations. Crown 8vo, cloth gilt, 2s. each.

"Nil Desperandum." By the Rev. F. Langbridge.

"Bear and Forbear." By Sarah Pitt.

"Foremost if I Can." By Helen Atteridge.

"Honour is my Guide." By Jeanie Hering (Mrs. Adams-Acton).

"Aim at the Sure End." By Emilie Searchfield.

"He Conquers who Endures." By the Author of "May Cunningham's Trial," &c.

The New Children's Album. Fcap. 4to, 320 pages. Illustrated throughout. 3s. 6d.

The History Scrap Book. With nearly 1,000 Engravings. 5s.; cloth, 7s. 6d.

"Little Folks" Half-Yearly Volume. With 200 Illustrations, 3s. 6d.; or cloth gilt, 5s.

Bo-Peep. A Book for the Little Ones. With Original Stories and Verses. Illustrated throughout. Boards, 2s. 6d.; cloth gilt, 3s. 6d.

The World's Lumber Room. By SELINA GAYE. Illustrated. 3s. 6d.

The "Proverbs" Series. Consisting of a New and Original Series of Stories by Popular Authors, founded on and illustrating well-known Proverbs. With Four Illustrations in each Book, printed on a tint. Crown 8vo, 160 pages, cloth, 1s. 6d. each.

Fritters; or, "It's a Long Lane that has no Turning." By Sarah Pitt.

Trixy; or, "Those who Live in Glass Houses shouldn't throw Stones." By Maggie Symington.

The Two Hardcastles; or, "A Friend in Need is a Friend Indeed." By Madeline Bonavia Hunt.

Major Monk's Motto; or, "Look Before you Leap." By the Rev. F. Langbridge.

Tim Thomson's Trial; or, "All is not Gold that Glitters." By George Weatherly.

Ursula's Stumbling-Block; or, "Pride comes before a Fall." By Julia Goddard.

Ruth's Life-Work; or, "No Pains, no Gains." By the Rev. Joseph Johnson.

The "Cross and Crown" Series. Consisting of Stories founded on incidents which occurred during Religious Persecutions of Past Days. With Four Illustrations in each Book, printed on a tint. Crown 8vo, 256 pages, 2s. 6d. each.

By Fire and Sword: a Story of the Huguenots. By Thomas Archer.

Adam Hepburn's Vow: a Tale of Kirk and Covenant. By Annie S. Swan.

No. XIII.; or, The Story of the Lost Vestal. A Tale of Early Christian Days. By Emma Marshall.

Selections from Cassell & Company's Publications.

The World's Workers. A Series of New and Original Volumes by Popular Authors. With Portraits printed on a tint as Frontispiece. 1s. each.

General Gordon. By the Rev. S. A. Swaine.
Charles Dickens. By his Eldest Daughter.
Sir Titus Salt and George Moore. By J. Burnley.
Florence Nightingale, Catherine Marsh, Frances Ridley Havergal, Mrs. Ranyard ("L. N. R.") By Lizzie Alldridge.
Dr. Guthrie, Father Mathew, Elihu Burritt, Joseph Livesey. By the Rev. J. W. Kirton.
Sir Henry Havelock and Colin Campbell, Lord Clyde. By E. C. Phillips.

Abraham Lincoln. By Ernest Foster.
David Livingstone. By Robert Smiles.
George Muller and Andrew Reed. By E. R. Pitman.
Richard Cobden. By R. Gowing.
Benjamin Franklin. By E. M. Tomkinson.
Handel. By Eliza Clarke.
Turner, the Artist. By the Rev. S. A. Swaine.
George and Robert Stephenson. By C. L. Mateaux.

The "Chimes" Series. Each containing 64 pages, with Illustrations on every page, and handsomely bound in cloth, 1s.

Bible Chimes. Contains Bible Verses for Every Day in the Month.
Daily Chimes. Verses from the Poets for Every Day in the Month.

Holy Chimes. Verses for Every Sunday in the Year.
Old World Chimes. Verses from old writers for Every Day in the Month.

New Five Shilling Books for Boys. With Original Illustrations, printed on a tint. Cloth gilt, 5s. each.

"Follow my Leader;" or, the Boys of Templeton. By Talbot Baines Reed.
For Fortune and Glory; a Story of the Soudan War. By Lewis Hough.

The Champion of Odin; or, Viking Life in the Days of Old. By J. Fred. Hodgetts.
Bound by a Spell; or, the Hunted Witch of the Forest. By the Hon. Mrs. Greene.

New Three and Sixpenny Books for Boys. With Original Illustrations, printed on a tint. Cloth gilt, 3s. 6d. each.

On Board the "Esmeralda;" or, Martin Leigh's Log. By John C. Hutcheson.
For Queen and King; or, the Loyal 'Prentice. By Henry Frith.

In Quest of Gold; or, Under the Whanga Falls. By Alfred St. Johnston.

The "Boy Pioneer" Series. By EDWARD S. ELLIS. With Four Full-page Illustrations in each Book. Crown 8vo, cloth, 2s. 6d. each.

Ned in the Woods. A Tale of Early Days in the West.
Ned in the Block House. A Story of Pioneer Life in Kentucky.
Ned on the River. A Tale of Indian River Warfare.

The "Log Cabin" Series. By EDWARD S. ELLIS. With Four Full-page Illustrations in each. Crown 8vo, cloth, 2s. 6d. each.

The Lost Trail.
Footprints in the Forest.
Camp-Fire and Wigwam.

Sixpenny Story Books. All Illustrated, and containing Interesting Stories by well-known Writers.

Little Content.
The Smuggler's Cave.
Little Lizzie.
Little Bird.
The Boot on the Wrong Foot.

Luke Barnicott.
Little Pickles.
The Boat Club.
The Elchester College Boys.
My First Cruise.

The Little Peacemaker.
The Delft Jug.
Lottie's White Frock.
Only Just Once.
Helpful Nellie; and other Stories.

The "Baby's Album" Series. Four Books, each containing about 50 Illustrations. Price 6d. each; or cloth gilt, 1s. each.

Baby's Album. | Dolly's Album. | Fairy's Album. | Pussy's Album.

Illustrated Books for the Little Ones. Containing interesting Stories. All Illustrated. 1s. each.

Indoors and Out.
Some Farm Friends.
Those Golden Sands.

Little Mothers and their Children.
Our Pretty Pets.

Our Schoolday Hours.
Creatures Tame.
Creatures Wild.

Shilling Story Books. All Illustrated, and containing Interesting Stories.

Thorns and Tangles.
The Cuckoo in the Robin's Nest.
John's Mistake.
Pearl's Fairy Flower.
Diamonds in the Sand.

The History of Five Little Pitchers.
Surly Bob.
The Giant's Cradle.
Shag and Doll.
Aunt Lucia's Locket.
A Banished Monarch.

The Magic Mirror.
The Cost of Revenge.
Clever Frank.
Among the Redskins.
The Ferryman of Brill.
Harry Maxwell.

Cassell's Children's Treasuries. Each Volume contains Stories or Poetry, and is profusely Illustrated. Cloth, 1s. each.

Cock Robin, and other Nursery Rhymes.
The Queen of Hearts.
Old Mother Hubbard.
Simple Rhymes for Happy Times.
Tuneful Lays for Merry Days.
Cheerful Songs for Young Folks.
Pretty Poems for Young People.

The Children's Joy.
Pretty Pictures and Pleasant Stories.
Our Picture Book.
Tales for the Little Ones.
My Sunday Book of Pictures.
Sunday Garland of Pictures and Stories.
Sunday Readings for Little Folks.

"Little Folks" Painting Books. With Text, and Outline Illustrations for Water-Colour Painting. 1s. each.

Fruits and Blossoms for "Little Folks" to Paint.
The "Little Folks" Proverb Painting Book.

The "Little Folks" Illuminating Book.
Pictures to Paint.
"Little Folks" Painting Book.
"Little Folks" Nature Painting Book.

Another "Little Folks" Painting Book.

Eighteenpenny Story Books. All Illustrated throughout.

Three Wee Ulster Lassies.
Little Queen Mab.
Up the Ladder.
Dick's Hero; and other Stories.
The Chip Boy.
Raggles, Baggles, and the Emperor.
Roses from Thorns.
Faith's Father.

By Land and Sea.
The Young Berringtons.
Jeff and Leff.
Tom Morris's Error.
Worth more than Gold.
"Through Flood—Through Fire;" and other Stories.
The Girl with the Golden Locks.

Stories of the Olden Time.

The "Cosy Corner" Series. Story Books for Children. Each containing nearly ONE HUNDRED PICTURES. 1s. 6d. each.

See-Saw Stories.
Little Chimes for All Times.
Wee Willie Winkie.
Pet's Posy of Pictures and Stories.
Dot's Story Book.

Story Flowers for Rainy Hours.
Little Talks with Little People.
Bright Rays for Dull Days.
Chats for Small Chatterers.
Pictures for Happy Hours.
Ups and Downs of a Donkey's Life.

The "World in Pictures" Series. Illustrated throughout. 2s. 6d. each.

A Ramble Round France.
All the Russias.
Chats about Germany.
The Land of the Pyramids (Egypt).
Peeps into China.

The Eastern Wonderland (Japan).
Glimpses of South America.
Round Africa.
The Land of Temples (India).
The Isles of the Pacific.

Two-Shilling Story Books. All Illustrated.

Stories of the Tower.
Mr. Burke's Nieces.
May Cunningham's Trial.
The Top of the Ladder: How to Reach it.
Little Flotsam.
Madge and her Friends.

The Children of the Court.
A Moonbeam Tangle.
Maid Marjory.
The Four Cats of the Tippertons.
Marion's Two Homes.
Little Folks' Sunday Book.

Two Fourpenny Bits.
Poor Nelly.
Tom Heriot.
Through Peril to Fortune.
Aunt Tabitha's Waifs.
In Mischief Again.

Half-Crown Books.

Little Hinges.
Margaret's Enemy.
Pen's Perplexities.
Notable Shipwrecks.
Golden Days.
Wonders of Common Things.
Little Empress Joan.
At the South Pole.

Truth will Out.
Pictures of School Life and Boyhood.
The Young Man in the Battle of Life. By the Rev. Dr. Landels.
The True Glory of Woman. By the Rev. Dr. Landels.
The Wise Woman. By George Macdonald.
Soldier and Patriot (George Washington).

Picture Teaching Series. Each book Illustrated throughout. Fcap. 4to, cloth gilt, coloured edges, 2s. 6d. each.

Through Picture-Land.
Picture Teaching for Young and Old.
Picture Natural History.
Scraps of Knowledge for the Little Ones.
Great Lessons from Little Things.

Woodland Romances.
Stories of Girlhood.
Frisk and his Flock.
Pussy Tip-Toes' Family.
The Boy Joiner and Model Maker.
The Children of Holy Scripture.

Library of Wonders. Illustrated Gift-books for Boys. 2s. 6d. each.

Wonderful Adventures.
Wonders of Animal Instinct.
Wonders of Architecture.
Wonders of Acoustics.

Wonders of Water.
Wonderful Escapes.
Bodily Strength and Skill.
Wonderful Balloon Ascents.

Gift Books for Children. With Coloured Illustrations. 2s. 6d. each.

The Story of Robin Hood.
Sandford and Merton.
Playing Trades.

True Robinson Crusoes. (Plain Illustrations.)
Reynard the Fox.

The Pilgrim's Progress.

The "Home Chat" Series. All Illustrated throughout. Fcap. 4to. Boards, 3s. 6d. each; cloth, gilt edges, 5s. each.

Home Chat.
Sunday Chats with Our Young Folks.
Peeps Abroad for Folks at Home.
Around and About Old England.

Half-Hours with Early Explorers.
Stories about Animals.
Stories about Birds.
Paws and Claws.

Books for the Little Ones.

The Little Doings of some Little Folks. By Chatty Cheerful. Illustrated. 5s.
The Sunday Scrap Book. With One Thousand Scripture Pictures. Boards, 5s.; cloth, 7s. 6d.
Daisy Dimple's Scrap Book. Containing about 1,000 Pictures. Boards, 5s.; cloth gilt, 7s. 6d.
Leslie's Songs for Little Folks. Illustrated. 1s. 6d.
The Little Folk's Out and About Book. By Chatty Cheerful. Illustrated. 5s.
Myself and my Friends. By Olive Patch. With numerous Illustrations. Crown 4to. 5s.
A Parcel of Children. By Olive Patch. With numerous Illustrations. Crown 4to. 5s.
Little Folks' Picture Album. With 168 Large Pictures. 5s.

Little Folks' Picture Gallery. With 150 Illustrations. 5s.
The Old Fairy Tales. With Original Illustrations. Boards, 1s.; cloth, 1s. 6d.
My Diary. With Twelve Coloured Plates and 366 Woodcuts. 1s.
Three Wise Old Couples. With 16 Coloured Plates. 5s.
Old Proverbs with New Pictures. With 24 Fac-simile Coloured Plates by Lizzie Lawson. The Text by C. L. Matéaux. 6s.
Happy Little People. By Olive Patch. With Illustrations. 5s.
"Little Folks" Album of Music, The. Illustrated. 3s. 6d.
Elfie Under the Sea. By E. L. Pearson. With Full-page Illustrations. 3s. 6d.

Books for Boys.

Kidnapped. By R. L. Stevenson.
The Phantom City. By W. Westall. 5s.
King Solomon's Mines. By H. Rider Haggard. 5s.
Famous Sailors of Former Times, being The Sea Fathers. By Clements Markham. Illustrated. 2s. 6d.
Treasure Island. By R. L. Stevenson. With Full-page Illustrations. 5s.

Modern Explorers. By Thomas Frost. Illustrated. 5s.
Cruise in Chinese Waters. By Capt. Lindley. Illustrated. 5s.
Wild Adventures in Wild Places. By Dr. Gordon Stables, M.D., R.N. Illustrated. 5s.
Jungle, Peak, and Plain. By Dr. Gordon Stables, R.N. Illustrated. 5s.
O'er Many Lands, on Many Seas. By Gordon Stables, M.D., R.N. Illustrated. 5s.

Books for all Children.

Cassell's Robinson Crusoe. With 100 striking Illustrations. Cloth, 3s. 6d.; gilt edges, 5s.
Cassell's Swiss Family Robinson. Illustrated. Cloth, 3s. 6d.; gilt edges, 5s.
Sunny Spain: Its People and Places, with Glimpses of its History. By Olive Patch. Illustrated. 5s.
Rambles Round London Town. By C. L. Matéaux. Illustrated. 5s.
Favorite Album of Fun and Fancy, The. Illustrated. 3s. 6d.
Familiar Friends. By Olive Patch. Illustrated. Cloth gilt, 5s.
Odd Folks at Home. By C. L. Matéaux. With nearly 150 Illustrations. 5s.
Field Friends and Forest Foes. By Olive Patch. Profusely Illustrated. 5s.

Silver Wings and Golden Scales. Illustrated. 5s.
The Wonderland of Work. By C. L. Matéaux. Illustrated. 7s. 6d.
Little Folks' Holiday Album. Illustrated. 3s. 6d.
Tiny Houses and their Builders. Illustrated. 5s.
Children of all Nations. Their Homes, their Schools, their Playgrounds. Illustrated. 5s.
Tim Trumble's "Little Mother." By C. L. Matéaux. Illustrated. 5s.
The Wonderland of Work. By C. L. Matéaux. Illustrated. 7s. 6d.
A Moonbeam Tangle. Original Fairy Tales. By Sydney Shadbolt. Illustrated. 3s. 6d.

CASSELL & COMPANY, Limited, *Ludgate Hill, London, Paris, New York and Melbourne.*

www.ingramcontent.com/pod-product-compliance
Lightning Source LLC
Chambersburg PA
CBHW032357020726
47499CB00008B/2789